[redacted]

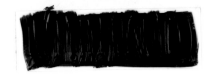

Libby Wimbley
GOAT TRAINER

by Amy Cobb   illustrated by Alexandria Neonakis

Calico Kid

An Imprint of Magic Wagon
abdopublishing.com

For Kassidy. Never change who YOU are! With special appreciation to Heidi for your kindness and encouragement. –AC

For John, Gooby and Kitty, whose love and support make my career possible. –AN

abdopublishing.com

Published by Magic Wagon, a division of ABDO, PO Box 398166, Minneapolis, Minnesota 55439. Copyright © 2018 by Abdo Consulting Group, Inc. International copyrights reserved in all countries. No part of this book may be reproduced in any form without written permission from the publisher. Calico Kid™ is a trademark and logo of Magic Wagon.

Printed in the United States of America, North Mankato, Minnesota.
052017
092017

THIS BOOK CONTAINS
RECYCLED MATERIALS

Written by Amy Cobb
Illustrated by Alexandria Neonakis
Edited by Heidi M.D. Elston
Art Directed by Laura Mitchell

Publisher's Cataloging-in-Publication Data

Names: Cobb, Amy, author. | Neonakis, Alexandria, illustrator.
Title: Goat trainer / by Amy Cobb ; illustrated by Alexandria Neonakis.
Description: Minneapolis, MN : Magic Wagon, 2018. | Series: Libby Wimbley
Summary: After attending her school's pet show, Libby is inspired to teach her
    goat, Elvis, some tricks. But Elvis won't catch a Frisbee. He nibbles on socks,
    rather than folding them. And he can't speak French. Then Libby has an idea.
    She realizes Elvis is already great at making friends and making people laugh.
    Elvis will make the perfect therapy goat!
Identifiers: LCCN 2017930829 | ISBN 9781532130250 (lib. bdg.) |
    ISBN 9781614798521 (ebook) | ISBN 9781614798576 (Read-to-me ebook)
Subjects: LCSH: Goats–Juvenile fiction. | Pet shows–Juvenile fiction. |
    Friendship–Juvenile fiction.
Classification: DDC [Fic]–dc23
LC record available at http://lccn.loc.gov/2017930829

Table of Contents

Chapter #1
Pet Show

Libby Wimbley and her friends were excited.

It was time for their school's annual fall festival. There were fun games. There were also cool prizes.

And there was Libby's favorite event. The pet show!

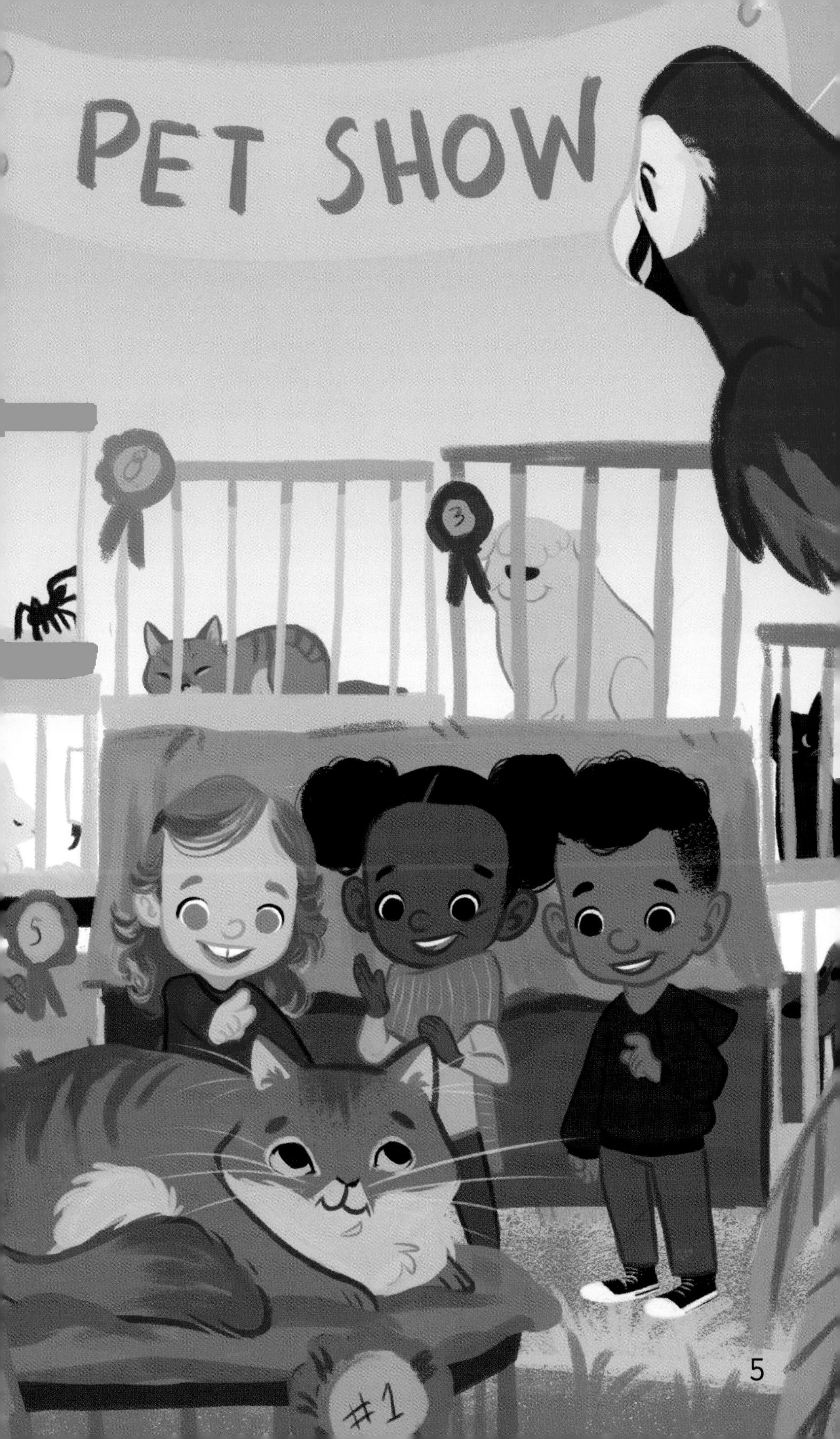
PET SHOW
3
5
#1

"Look at that cat!" Becca said. "I didn't know cats could catch Frisbees."

"Me neither. But my favorite animal is the dog that folds socks with her nose," said Mason.

Libby smiled. "I wish I had a dog like that when it's time to sort my laundry!"

Becca and Mason laughed.

Then Mason asked, "What's your favorite animal, Libby?"

Libby thought for a minute. She wasn't sure.

There was the goldfish that swam through a tiny hoop.

And the colorful parrot that said, "Bonjour!" Libby had never heard a parrot say hello in French before.

"I like them all," Libby finally said.
"But none of them are as smart as
Elvis."

"Your goat?" Becca asked.

Libby nodded. Then she got an
idea. Maybe she could teach Elvis
some tricks. Her friends could help.

Chapter #2
Serious Business

On Saturday, Becca and Mason went to the farm where Libby lived. They found Libby in the pasture with Elvis.

"Hello!" Libby waved. "You're just in time to see the goat trainer extraordinaire in action."

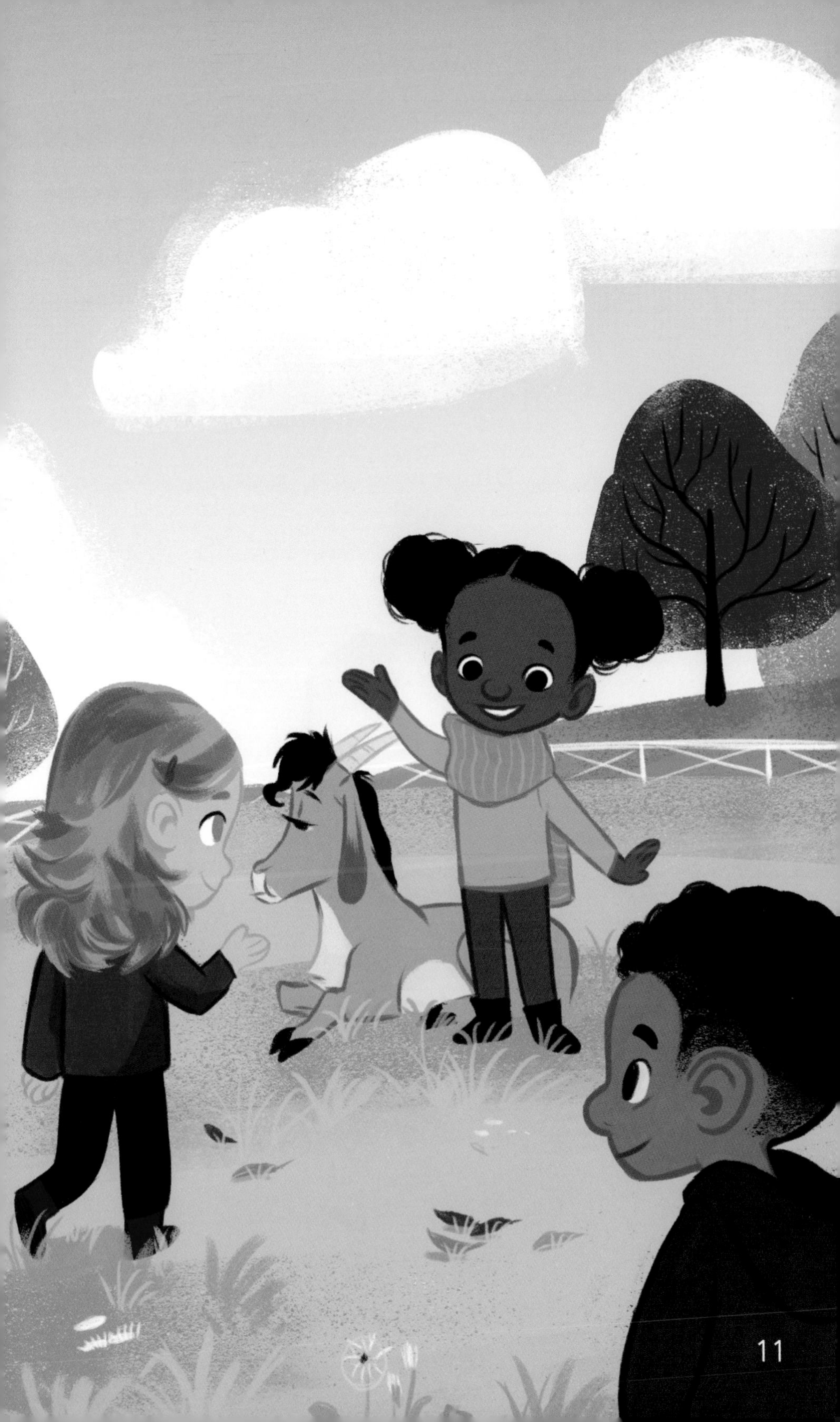

Becca and Mason both smiled.

"What trick will you teach Elvis first?" Becca asked.

Libby held up a Frisbee. "Let's show Elvis how to play."

Libby tossed the Frisbee to Mason. Then Mason threw it to Becca. When Becca caught it, she sailed it back through the air to Libby.

"See, Elvis? It's easy," Libby said. "Catch!"

But Elvis didn't catch the Frisbee. It flew right past his horns and landed with a thud on the grass. Elvis pawed it with his hooves.

"I don't think Elvis likes the Frisbee," Mason said.

Libby shrugged. "Let's try another trick. The dog at the pet show folded socks. I bet Elvis can, too."

She pulled a pair of socks from her pocket. But Elvis began nibbling on them.

Becca and Mason laughed. But Libby didn't. Being a goat trainer extraordinaire was serious business.

Chapter #3
Silly Goat

Libby tried a different trick. "Elvis, say bonjour!" She even held up an apple slice for a treat.

But Elvis couldn't speak French like the bird at the school pet show. He only spoke goat.

Meh-meh, he said, reaching for the apple.

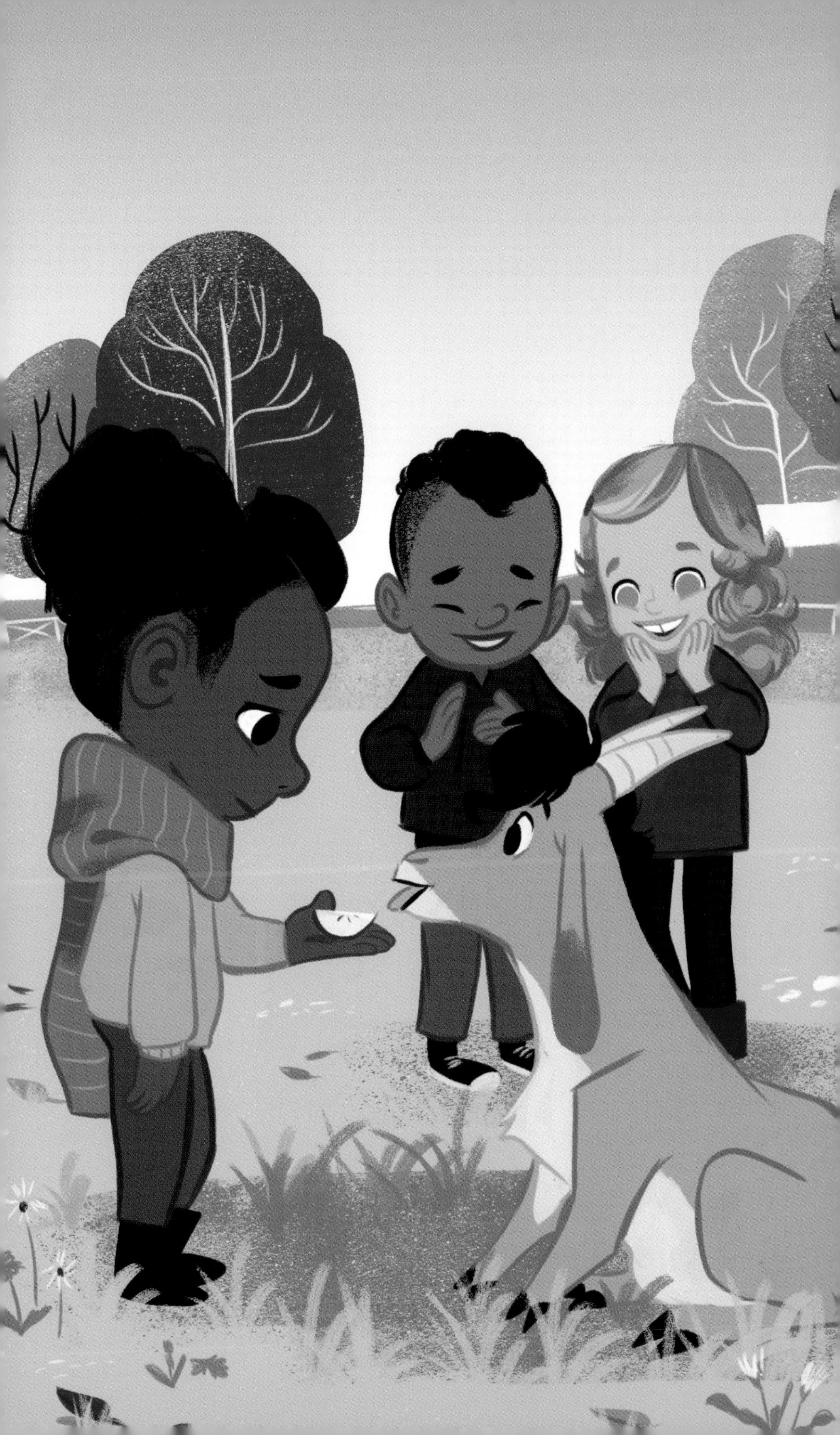

"Maybe you should try an easy trick," Becca said.

Mason nodded. "Like sit. Or stay."

"Good idea!" Libby said.

But Elvis wouldn't sit. And when Libby told Elvis to stay, he didn't.

Instead, Elvis followed Libby everywhere she went.

"Let's take a break," Libby said.

She and her friends sat on the cool grass.

"Elvis must be good at something," Mason said.

"But what?" Libby picked at a dandelion leaf. She was sad that Elvis might never star in a pet show.

Elvis began to nuzzle Libby's hair. Then her cheek.

"Stop it, silly goat!" Libby laughed and petted him.

Mason smiled. "Elvis is funny."

"And he loves people," Becca said when Elvis climbed onto her lap.

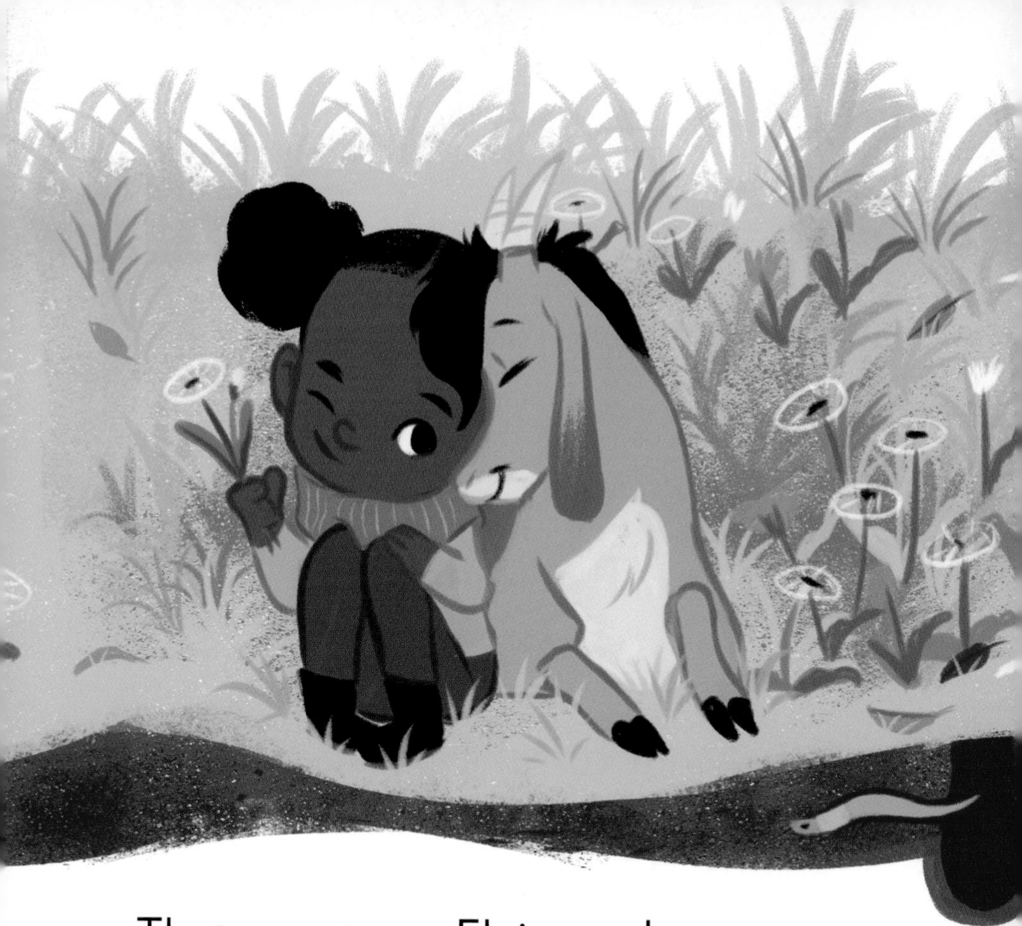

That was true. Elvis made everyone laugh. And he liked making friends.

"That's it!" Libby cried.

"Is it a new trick for Elvis?" Becca asked.

"Sort of," Libby said. "You'll see soon."

Chapter 4

Big News

Later that day, Becca and Mason went home. Then Libby told her family about her new idea.

"You want to take Elvis to visit elderly people in retirement centers?" Mom asked.

"Right." Libby nodded. "And people in hospitals. Plus, kids at school, too."

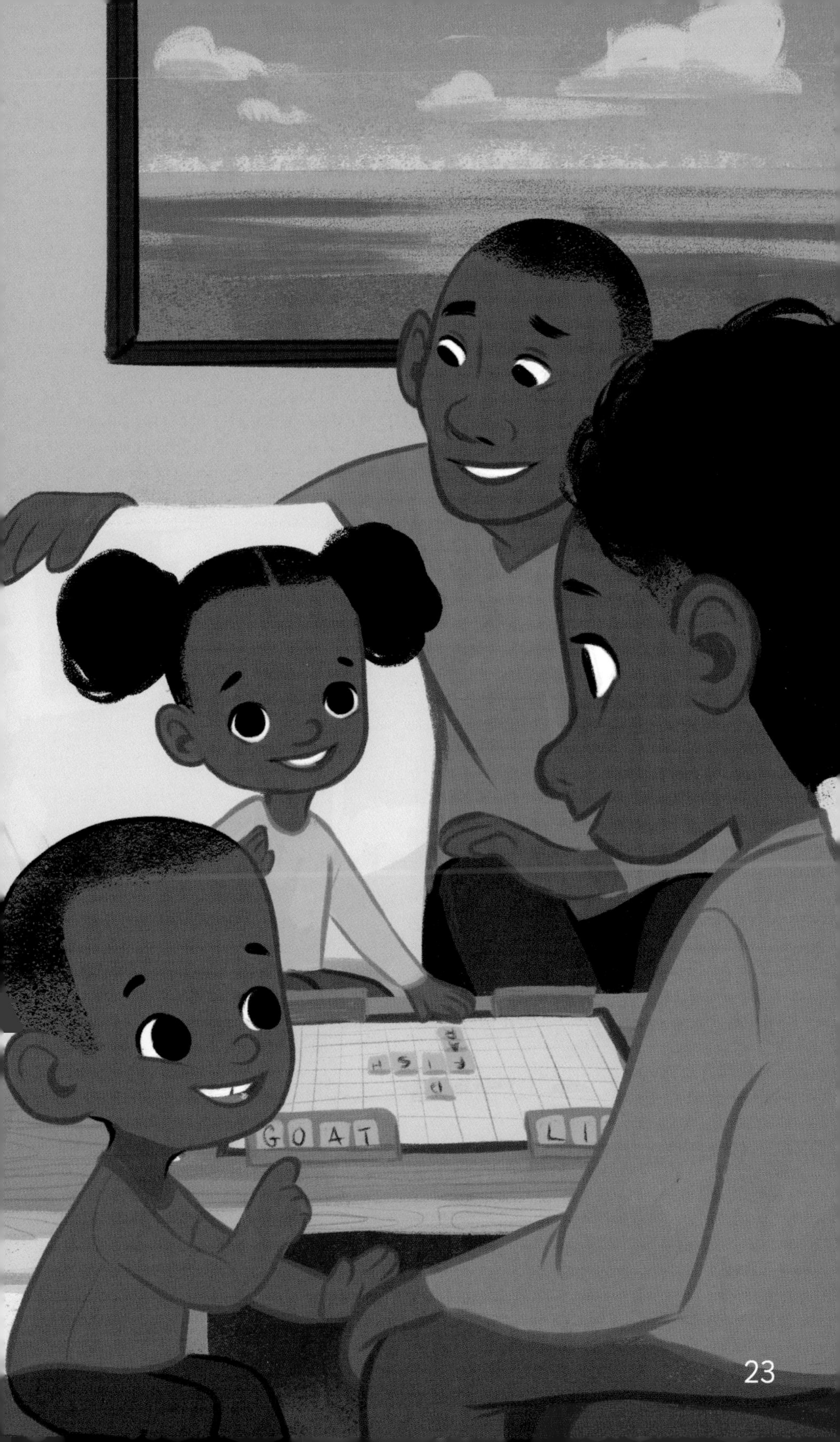
GOAT

Dad said, "I've heard of dogs doing that."

"But Elvis isn't a dog," Libby's brother, Stewart, said.

"Of course, he isn't," Libby said. "That's the best part. Wouldn't it be cool to see a goat at school?"

Stewart laughed. "Hey, that rhymes! And I guess it would be cool."

"Super cool!" Libby said, smiling.

So Mom and Dad helped Libby make some phone calls. When they were finished, Elvis had lots of places to visit.

Libby held up the calendar. "For the next few weeks, Elvis is going to be a busy goat," she said.

"And you'll be a busy girl," Dad said. "Elvis is your goat. So you have to go with him."

Dad was right. Libby and Elvis would make new friends together.

"I can't wait until Elvis hears the big news!" Libby said. She rushed outside to tell him.

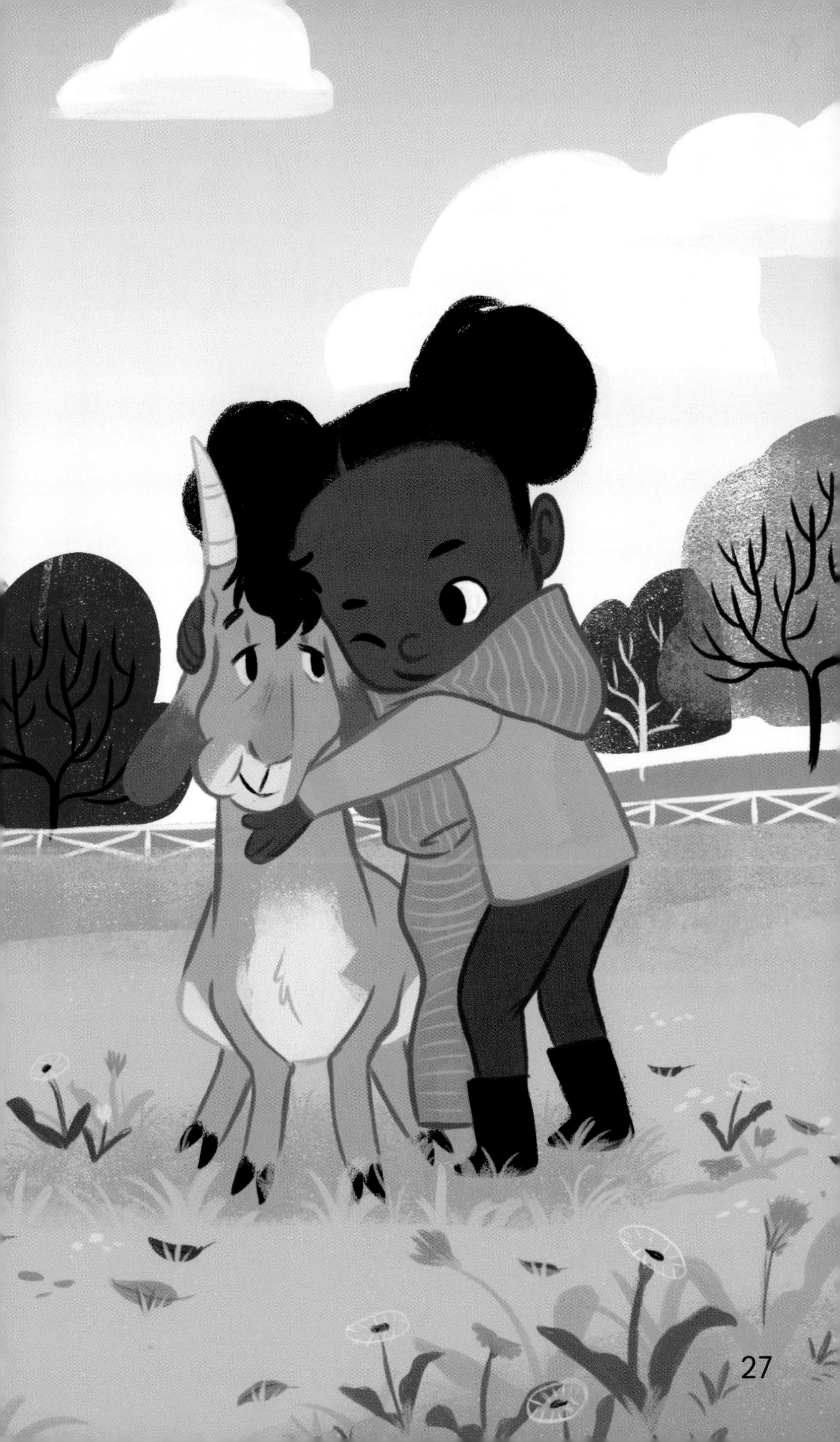

Chapter #5
One Special Goat

The first place Libby and Elvis went was the retirement center. Everyone there petted Elvis and fed him treats.

A few days later, they visited the hospital. Elvis snuggled with the patients.

The nurses asked Libby to bring Elvis back again.

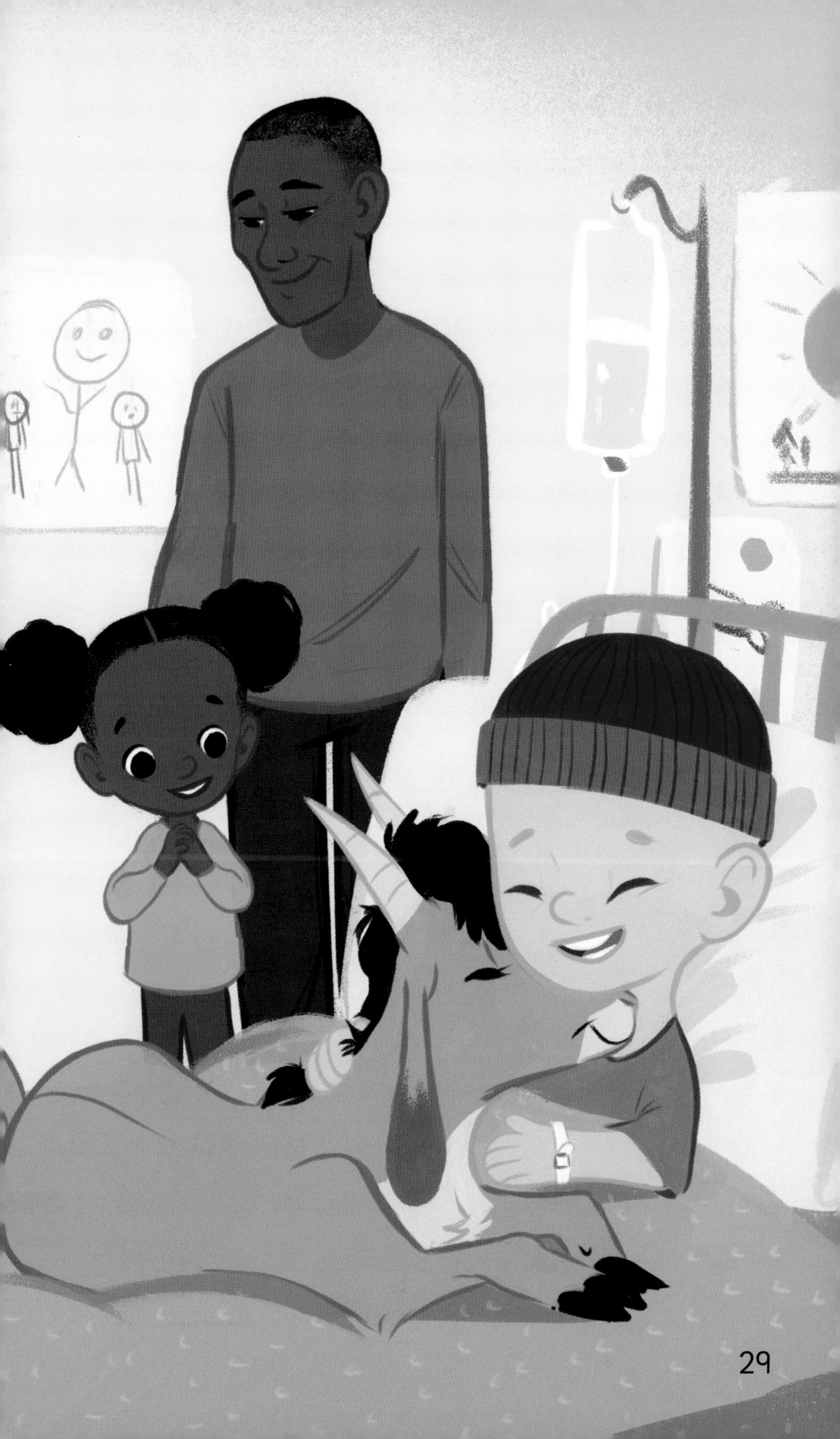

Now Libby and Elvis were at Libby's school.

Lots of kids gathered around Elvis. They took turns reading books to him.

Elvis sniffed the pages and said, *Meh-meh*!

Becca and Mason were there, too.

"I think Elvis is a hit," Becca said.

"Maybe the kids will teach Elvis to read," Mason said. "That would be a good trick."

Libby laughed. "It would be. But Elvis isn't a trick goat, after all. He's a therapy goat!"

"A therapy goat?" Becca asked.

And Mason said, "Are you serious?"

Libby was serious. It turned out Elvis didn't need to learn tricks, like catching a Frisbee or sorting socks.

Elvis was best at just being himself. Libby thought Elvis was one special goat.

"Sure!" Libby finally said. "And it has a nice ring to it. Elvis, the therapy goat extraordinaire!"